MW01258741

Reycraft Books
55 Fifth Avenue
New York, NY 10003

Reycraftbooks.com

Reycraft Books is a trade imprint and trademark of Newmark Learning, LLC.

This edition is published by arrangement with China Children's Press & Publication Group, China.
© China Children's Press & Publication Group

All rights reserved. No portion of this book may be reproduced, stored in a retrieval system, or transmitted in any form or by any means, electronic, mechanical, photocopying, recording, or otherwise, without written permission from the publisher. For information regarding permission, please contact info@reycraftbooks.com.

Educators and Librarians: Our books may be purchased in bulk for promotional, educational, or business use. Please contact sales@reycraftbooks.com.

This is a work of fiction. Names, characters, places, dialogue, and incidents described either are the product of the author's imagination or are used fictitiously. Any resemblance to actual persons, living or dead, is entirely coincidental.

Sale of this book without a front cover or jacket may be unauthorized. If this book is coverless, it may have been reported to the publisher as "unsold or destroyed" and may have deprived the author and publisher of payment.

Library of Congress Cataloging-in-Publication Data is available.

ISBN: 978-1-4788-6873-6

Printed in Guangzhou, China
4401/0919/CA21901491

10 9 8 7 6 5 4 3 2 1

First Edition Paperback published by Reycraft Books 2019

Reycraft Books and Newmark Learning, LLC, support diversity and the First Amendment, and celebrate the right to read.

A Pouch for Pocket

written by RAN YI
illustrated by YONGHENG WEI

On a big, grassy grassland lived a little blue kangaroo named Pocket.

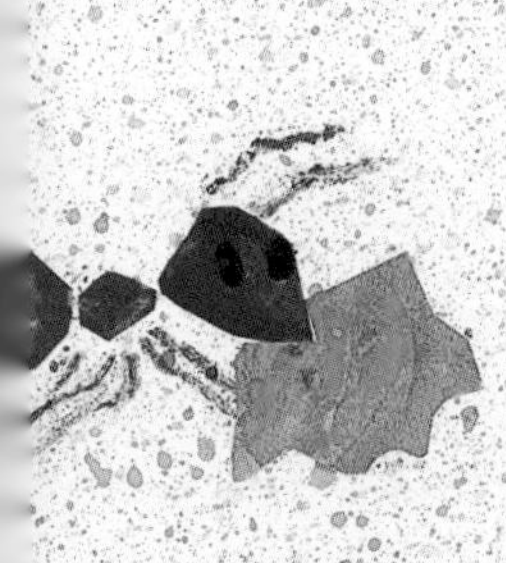

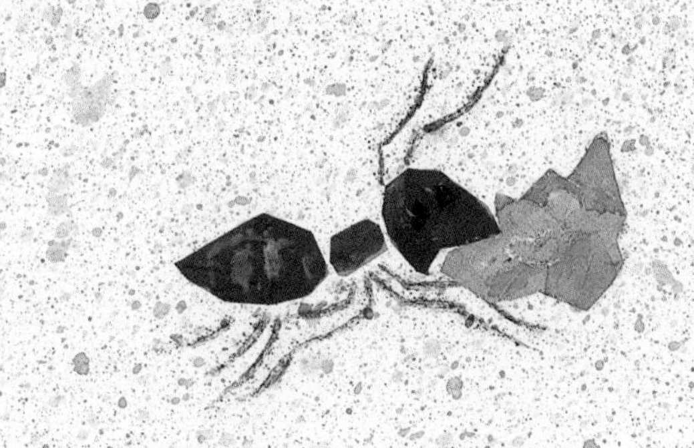

Pocket loved to hop
high in the air.

She knew all about hopping.

What she **didn't** know was why she had a pouch on her tummy.

One day, Pocket hopped through a field of flowers.

BOING!

"Wait a minute," said Pocket.

"Maybe my pouch is a vase."

But as soon as the wind blew,

most of the flowers

flew out.

And the ones that stayed
wilted
in the hot sun.

This was **not** what a pouch was for.

Pocket hopped across a river.

BOING!

Suddenly, a little fish jumped

right into her pouch.

"Wait a minute,"
said Pocket.

"Maybe my pouch is a **fishbowl.**"

But as soon as she stood,

all the water splashed out

and the fish jumped back into the river.

This was **not** what a pouch was for.

Pocket hopped up to a beehive.

Yum!

"Wait a minute,"
said Pocket.

"Maybe my pouch is a honey jar."

But not only was the honey

stickystickysticky,

the bees wanted it, too.

Uh-oh!

Pocket hopped away
as fast as she could.

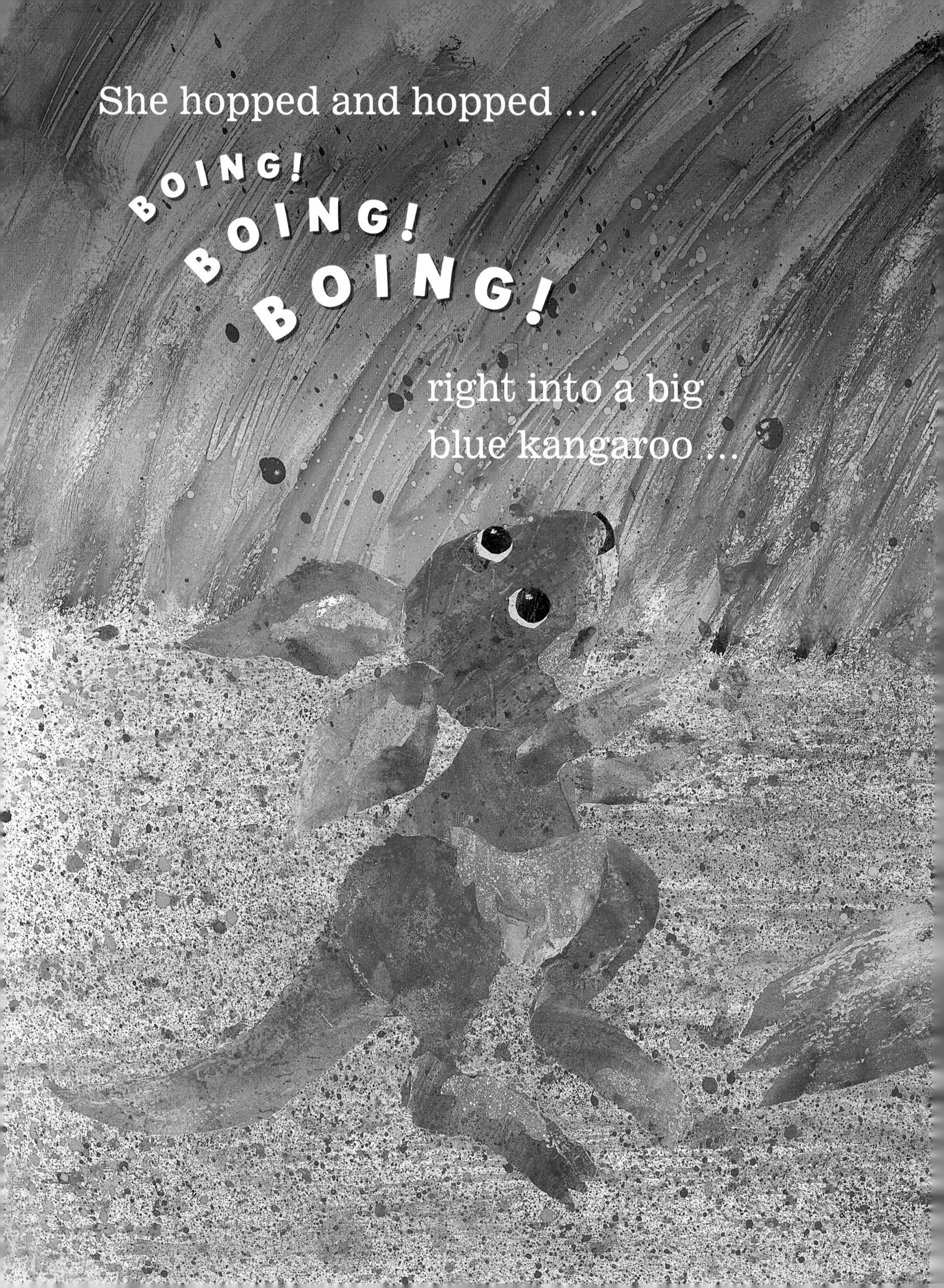
She hopped and hopped ...
BOING!
BOING!
BOING!
right into a big
blue kangaroo ...

who happened
to be her Mama.

“Quick! Jump into my pouch,” said Mama.

Mama Kangaroo hopped

great big hops,

leaving those bees behind.

And Pocket fell asleep

in Mama's safe, warm pouch.

Mama Kangaroo patted
her pouch and said,

"My pouch is your **home,** little Pocket."

"Oh, I see,"
said Pocket.

"**This** is what a pouch is for!"

RAN YI

was a passionate advocate of childhood reading and the founder of the Little Book Room children's literacy organization. She was also a translator and a literacy writer and educator.

YONGHENG WEI

is a well-known illustrator and the creative force behind two popular Chinese publications: a parenting magazine and a magazine for children and babies.